HOTSHOTS!

CHRIS L. DEMAREST

Margaret K. McElderry Books

NEW YORK · LONDON · TORONTO · SYDNEY · SINGAPORE

For Emma Dryden,
who saw, through the smoke, the story
I desperately wanted to tell

With special thanks to Chuck Sheley of the National Smokejumpers Association
and Jim Litevich, Executive Director, Vermont Fire Service Training

Margaret K. McElderry Books
An imprint of Simon & Schuster Children's Publishing Division
1230 Avenue of the Americas, New York, New York 10020

The text of this book is set in HTF Champion.
The illustrations for this book are rendered in pastels.

Manufactured in China
2 4 6 8 10 9 7 5 3 1
Library of Congress Cataloging-in-Publication Data
Demarest, Chris L.
Hotshots! / Chris L. Demarest.
p. cm.
Summary: Rhyming text introduces the equipment and work of a team of fire fighters
as they battle a blaze caused by a spark from a train. Includes bibliographical references.
ISBN 0-689-84816-1
1. Forest fire fighters—Juvenile literature. [1. Forest fire fighters. 2. Wildfires.] I. Title.
SD421.23 .D45 2003
634.9'618—dc21
2002002695

FIRST
EDITION

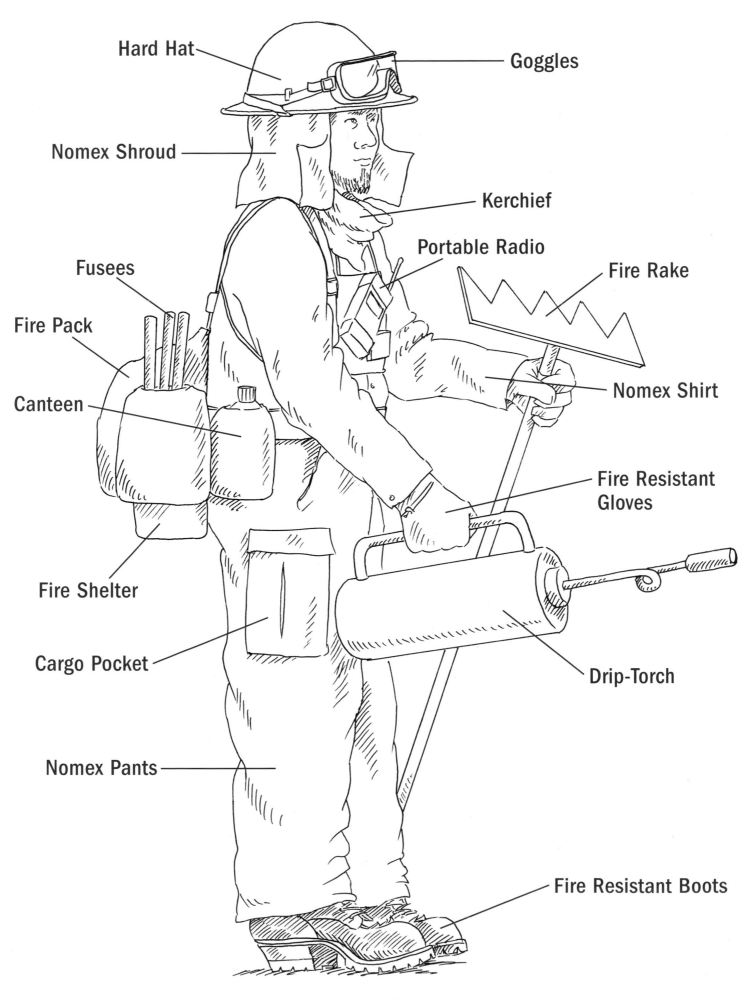

Hard Hat

Goggles

Nomex Shroud

Kerchief

Portable Radio

Fire Rake

Fusees

Fire Pack

Nomex Shirt

Canteen

Fire Resistant Gloves

Fire Shelter

Drip-Torch

Cargo Pocket

Nomex Pants

Fire Resistant Boots

Hotshot Outfit

Sparks from a train ignite a field baked for days.

Then winds whip it into a fast-running blaze.

With fire now spreading out of control,

the hotshots are called. They're ready to roll.

On brush rigs and trucks, they head to the scene . . .

. . . where fire's now climbing up deep ravines.

For some people's homes, it is just much too late.

Chaparral explodes and jumps a side street.

A wood-shingled roof torches off from the heat.

While structural crews fight one raging battle, . . .

. . . the hotshots race up to the ridge-top saddle.

A skycrane swoops down to drop its water load,

but fire jumps effortlessly over the road.

With drip-torches and fusees, 'shots race through scrub grass.

A "four-fifteen" bucks through thick smoke on a pass.

Fighting fire with fire, hotshots create a backburn

and hope the wind-driven fire won't suddenly turn.

While one crew digs a line off to the right flank,

a second scrapes dirt on the opposite bank.

as flames spiral sixty feet into the air.

The hotshots drop tools and deploy "Shake 'n Bakes"

as fire races up, heading straight for the break.

A deafening roar. Shelters snap violently.

Winds blast the tents' sides with burning debris.

The 'shots' faces stay pressed to the ground.
The fire attacks.

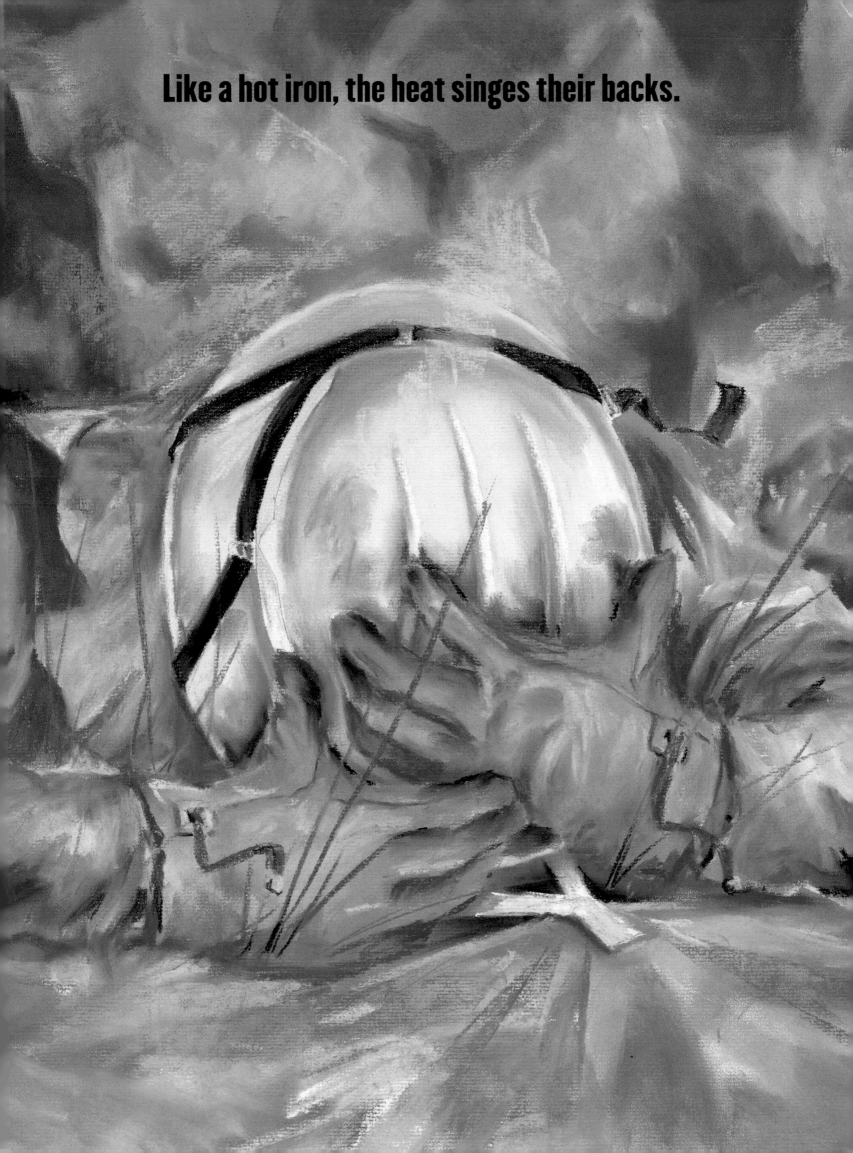
Like a hot iron, the heat singes their backs.

It's suddenly quiet. There's calm all about.

The backburn has worked. The fire is out.

Time to reload tools and grab a quick bite,

for the hotshots know there's more fire to fight.

AUTHOR'S NOTE

Whenever we hear about wildfires, we hear about the "hotshots" who battle these blazes. Far from a generic term for forest firefighters, hotshots are the elite ground firefighting corps with permanent stations dotted throughout the western United States.

Hotshots are trained to understand the scientific characteristics of fire. Fire is affected by many conditions: weather, topography (the ground slope of the fire area), and the amount of fuel that's available to feed the fire. Armed only with tools they can carry—shovels and rakes, chain saws and half hoe/half axe tools known as Pulaskis—these men and women work to stop a fire by creating a break in its path. They make a three-to-five-foot-wide path around the perimeter of the blaze by cutting down trees, removing small plants and brush, and then scraping the ground down to bare earth, thereby robbing the fire of the fuel it needs to feed itself.

Another method hotshots use to stop a fire from spreading is to create a "backburn," or "burnout." The hotshots light a line of fire ahead of the oncoming main blaze. Using a variety of incendiary devices, such as fusees (which resemble flares) and drip-torches (handheld canisters that drip a mixture of burning gasoline and diesel oil), the hotshots set new fires parallel to the wildfire. The new fires burn toward the main fire, creating an area called a "good black," which is devoid of fuel. When the wildfire hits the "good black," it will be stopped in its tracks with nothing to feed on.

Even with many years of experience, a hotshot can be caught by a fast-moving fire. If it's impossible to get to "good black," the hotshot must deploy a fire shelter pulled from their pack or waistband. Known in the fire service as a "Shake 'n Bake," this small, frameless, aluminum-skin tent is pinned down on the ground over a hotshot's body by his or her hands and feet. The "Shake 'n Bake" offers about two minutes of protection against the thousand-degree temperature outside.

Hotshots do not fight fires alone. On the ground, bulldozers are used to make a quick fire break. From the air, everything from fire-retardant liquid to water is dropped on or in front of the fire. Small helicopters drop water from a "Bambi bucket." Larger choppers, such as skycranes, use a long hose to suck up water into a holding tank. With the touch of a button the water can be released directly onto the fire. Most airplanes load water or fire-retardant liquid at an air base and then fly to the site of the fire. A Canadair "415" and other amphibious aircraft can refill their tanks in less than a minute by skimming the surface of a water source—such as a lake or large pond—near the fire.

Traditionally, hotshots mostly fought wildfires in heavily forested areas, but they are now being called to fight fires closer to towns and cities as well. As cities in some parts of the United States (particularly on the West Coast) have expanded into the surrounding hills, highly flammable material has been added to the wild landscape. Homes and other structures built into this vegetation become a volatile fuel source for an out-of-control fire. This is referred to as an urban interface fire.

The hotshots' season can start in early spring to assist fire suppression in Florida and last into the fall in the Southwest. Many wilderness fires are started by natural phenomena, such as lightning striking a tree. But many fires are man-made. As the fire season progresses and the landscape dries, little is needed to start fires. Unfortunately, carelessness is the main cause of many of these fires.

As deadly and dangerous as fires are, the men and women who work as hotshots live to face the challenge of fighting fires. This is a job they love to do. This is a job they live to do.

—C. L. D.

Suggested Reading and Viewing

Buckley, John A. *Hotshot.* Boulder, Colorado: Pruett Publishing Company, 1990.

California Firestorm '96. Produced by Alan Simmons and John P. Harris. 65 min. 1996. Videocassette.

Firestorm: The Smokejumpers' Story. 104 min. Bethesda, M.D.: The Discovery Channel, 1999. Videocassette.

Maclean, John N. *Fire on the Mountain: The True Story of the South Canyon Fire.* New York: William Morrow and Company, 1999.

Thoele, Michael. *Fire Line: The Summer Battles of the West.* Golden, Colorado: Fulcrum Publishing, 1995.

Suggested Web Sites

www.smokeybear.com
www.wildlandfirefighter.net
www.usfa.fema.gov
www.fs.fed.us